Mary Had a Little

Mary had a little lamb,

Its fleece was white as snow;

And everywhere that Mary went,

the lamb was sure to go.

It followed her to school one day,

Which was against the rule;

It made the children laugh and play,

To see a lamb at school.

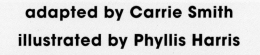

adapted by Carrie Smith

illustrated by Phyllis Harris

I see the house.

I see the girl.

I see the bag.

I see the school.

I see the classroom.

I see the teacher.

I see the students.

I see the lamb!